A NOTE TO PARENTS

Early Step into Reading Books are designed for preschoolers and kindergartners who are just getting ready to read. The words are easy, the type is big, and the stories are packed with rhyme, rhythm, and repetition.

We suggest that you read this book to your child the first few times, pointing to each word as you go. Soon your child will start saying the words with you. And before long, he or she will try to read the story alone. Don't be surprised if your child uses the pictures to figure out the text—that's what they're there for! The important thing is to develop your child's confidence—and to show your child that reading is fun.

When your child is ready to move on, try the rest of the steps in our Step into Reading series. **Step 1 Books** (preschool–grade 1) feature the same easy-to-read type as the Early Step into Reading Books, but with more words per page. **Step 2 Books** (grades 1–3) are both longer and slightly more difficult, while **Step 3 Books** (grades 2–3) introduce readers to paragraphs and fully developed plot lines. **Step 4 Books** (grades 2–4) offer exciting nonfiction for the increasingly independent reader.

The grade levels assigned to the five steps are intended only as guides. Some children move through all five steps very rapidly; others climb the steps over a period of several years. Either way, these books will help your child "step into reading" in style!

http://www.randomhouse.com/

Library of Congress Cataloging-in-Publication Data
Cobb, Annie. B is for books! / by Annie Cobb ; illustrated by Joe Mathieu.
p. cm. — (Early step into reading) "Featuring Jim Henson's Sesame Street Muppets."
SUMMARY: Oscar's pet worm Slimey describes some of the many subjects that can be found in books.
ISBN 0-679-86446-6 (pbk.) — ISBN 0-679-96446-0 (lib. bdg.) [1. Books and reading—Fiction.
2. Puppets—Fiction. 3. Stories in rhyme.] I. Mathieu, Joseph, ill. II. Title. III. Series. PZ8.3.C625Baai
1996 [E]—dc20 96-11142
Printed in the United States of America 10 9 8 7 6 5 4 3 2 1
STEP INTO READING is a trademark of Random House, Inc.

Early Step into Reading™

B is for Books!

By Annie Cobb

Illustrated by Joe Mathieu

Featuring Jim Henson's Sesame Street Muppets

Random House/Children's Television Workshop

B is for books.
All kinds of books.

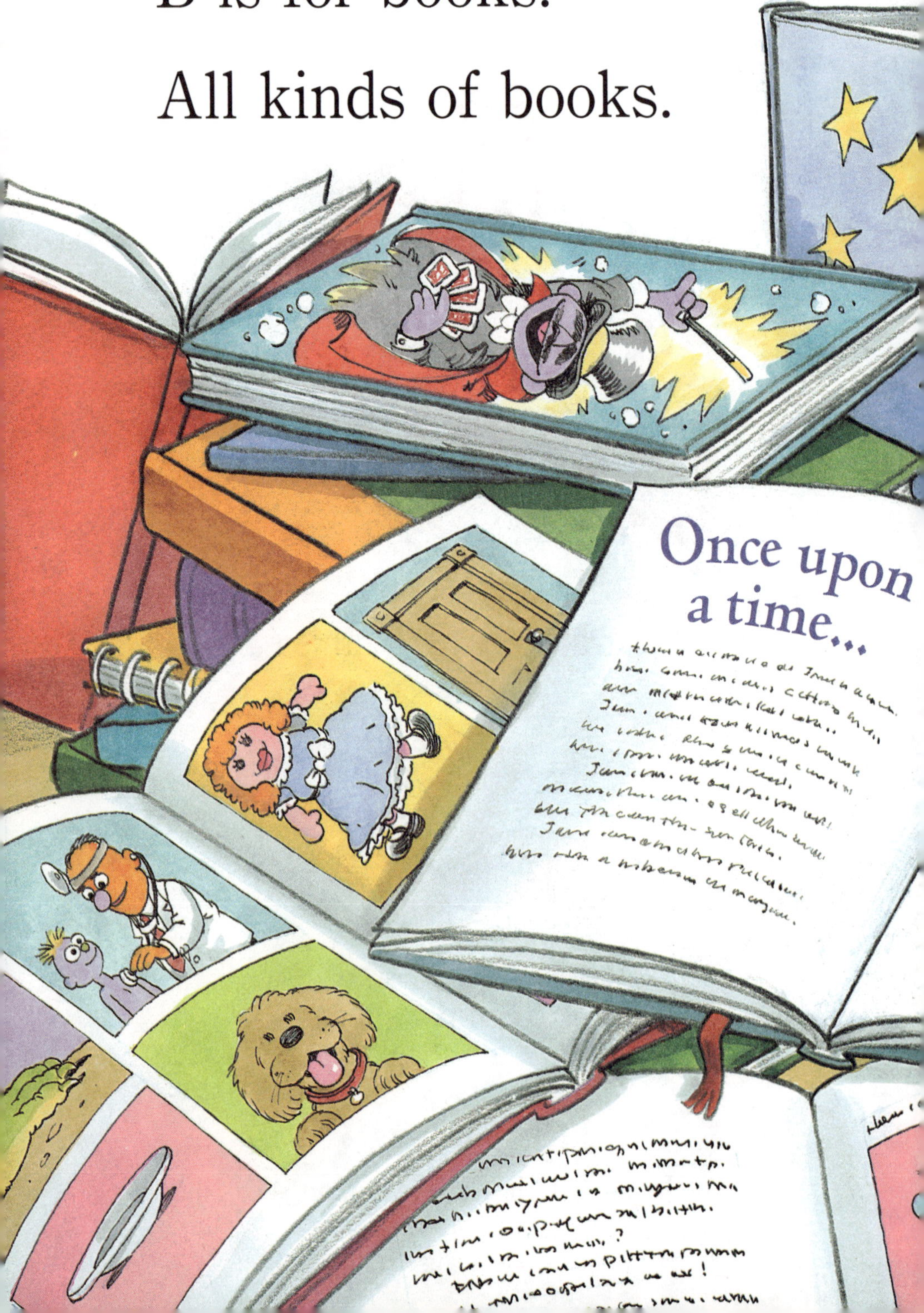
Once upon a time...

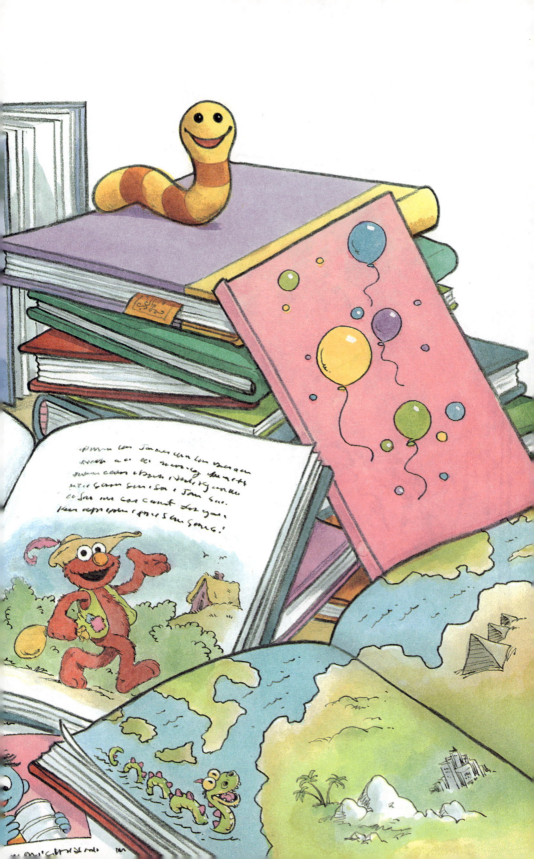

Books about counting.

Books about cooks.

Books about blue things.

Books about birds.

July 4, 1776

Books about true things.

Books about words.

wagon

wrap

whale

worm

Books about bodies.

hair

head

hand

ear

elbow

arm

belly
button

head

body

leg

foot

Books about beads.

Books about magic.

Books about weeds.

Books full of poems.

Rain, rain, go away.

Come again another day.

Books full of maps.

Books good for playtime.

Books good for naps.

Rock-a-bye baby, on the treetop.

Books full of stories.

Books full of stars.

Books full of riddles.

And books are for me!

B is for books.

Once upon
a time...

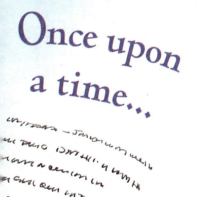

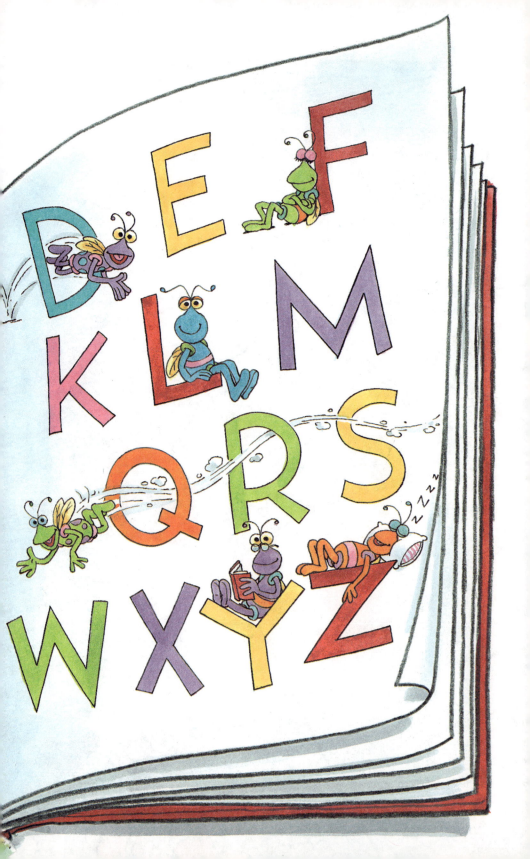

Books about letters
from A to Z.

Books full of cars.